W I N D O W S
of H E A V E N

by

Idell LaVette Gatterson

DORRANCE
PUBLISHING CO
EST. 1920
PITTSBURGH, PENNSYLVANIA 15238

Dorrance Publishing Co
585 Alpha Drive
Suite 103
Pittsburgh, PA 15238
Visit our website at *www.dorrancebookstore.com*

ISBN: 978-1-6453-0765-5
eISBN: 978-1-6461-0952-4

Windows of Heaven
VOICE OF GOD

Location
Dixie, Louisiana
(circa 1950s)

SCENE 1

Camera pans over countryside at night showing the title "Windows of Heaven" across movie screen. It is night (the weekend). Dad and some of his friends decide to go to the Gambling Shack. Dad leaves home and meets his friend near the tree by the window. Dad arrives at friends' house, picks him up, and go to the Gambling Shack.

                         DAD

        We're here.

                      FRIEND 1

        Tonight is my night!

                         DAD

        I don't gamble.

                  FRIEND 1 (SHOUTS)

        Anybody want some of this game?

                      FRIEND 2

        Yes, I'm in.

They commence to gamble. Friend 1 wins the game.

                      FRIEND 1

        I won — pay up!

FRIEND 2

No, I don't owe you anything

FRIEND 1

Look pal, I won the game

Friend 2 is silent.

DAD (CONFUSED)

Pay him so we can go back home

FRIEND 2

No! I'm not paying him!

Dad and Friend 1 leave the scene. They go to Friend 1's house. Dad's friend goes into his house, retrieves a gun, and returns back to the scene. Friend 1 opens fire and shoots Friend 2 to death.

FRIEND 1 (TO DAD)

Let's go! Take me home.

DAD

Okay.

FRIEND 1

If anyone ask you if I killed the man—you better not tell.

DAD

Okay.

Scene 2

Friend 2 lies in blood at the Gambling Shack near the tree by the window. The patrons at the Gambling Shack call the police. The police arrive at the scene, and Friend 2 is dead on arrival. Patron 1 address the police.

Patron 1

Officer, I saw the man who shot him. They were driving a '58 Chevy license plate number 321 CBA.

The police get in the car and pull up the car's registration. The car is registered in Dad's name. The policemen arrive at Dad's mother's house. They knock on the door. MaDear, Dad's mother, answers the door.

MaDear

Hello officers. Is there a problem?

Police 1

Yeah there is a problem. There was a shooting at the Gambling Shack. Your son and another man were involved and left the scene. A man was shot and killed at the Gambling Shack.

Police 2

Can we talk to your son?

MaDear

Yes. Let me get him.

MaDear goes to her son's room. He is in bed sweating profusely and is shaking

MADEAR

Son, get up. The police is at the door.

DAD

Yes sir, may I help you?

POLICE 2

Where have you been tonight?

DAD

The Gambling Shack.

POLICE 1

You were seen at the Gambling Shack. A man was shot and killed.
You and another man left the scene.

POLICE 2

Who shot the man?

DAD (NERVOUS)

Why are you asking me? I did not shoot the man.

POLICE 1

Well, who shot him?

Dad is silent.

POLICE 2

Tell us what you saw.

DAD

I saw something.

POLICE 1

If you won't cooperate, I'm going to take you to jail.

DAD (SHAKING)

Okay, okay. My friend shot and killed the man.

The policemen leave the house. They go to Friend 1's house and arrest him. They read him his rights and handcuff him.

FRIEND 1 (ANGRILY)

I did not shoot the man. Who told you I shot and killed him?

POLICE 1

We will follow this up in court.

Meanwhile, Dad and MaDear are at home talking near the tree by the window.

MADEAR

I told you to stay at home with your wife and kids. Now you are going to have to testify in court. Trouble — nothing but trouble!

DAD

Yes MaDear. After I get out of this, I promise I won't disobey you again.

It is still night. Dad's wife and kids are sleep. MaDear and Dad stay up the entire night. The sun rises near the tree by the window, and it is morning. Dad is nervous, sweating profusely, and is afraid.

MaDear

You don't look so well. I'm taking you to the hospital.

Dad

Okay. I am not feeling well.

SCENE 3

In the courtroom near the tree by the window. Inside courtroom is Dad, his wife, and MaDear. Along with Friend 1, the Gambling Shack patrons, and the judge/jury. Court is in session.

PROSECUTOR (TO DAD)

Did Friend 1 shoot him in cold blood?

DAD (ANSWERS)

Yes.

Friend 1 is handcuffed and taken to prison. He resists being handcuffed.

FRIEND 1 (SHOUTS)

I told you not to tell. I'm coming after you!

Dad cries with his head in his hands. They leave the courtroom back to MaDear's house near the tree by the window.

MADEAR

I am taking you to the hospital for help.

DAD (SWEATING PROFUSELY)

Okay.

MaDear and Dad goes to the hospital to be seen by a psychiatrist. Dad stays in hospital without a diagnosed illness. Dad is shaking with a whole-body spasm with tremoring hands. Later in the evening, Dad begins to have flash blacks about his youth.

SCENE 4

In Dixie, Louisiana along the dirt road surrounded by Bradford Pear Trees in an open field, Dad and his dad is at work on a tractor trailer with other workers.

DAD'S FATHER

Cut and clear the trees down.

Dad, Dad's Father, and workers clear the Bradford Pear Trees until evening. At the end of the day, they go home. It is the weekend. On Sunday morning, the whole family goes to church.

DAD'S FATHER

Let's go. It's time for church.

MADEAR

All right. Come on kids!

At church, Dad's Father waits outside the church and does not go in. He waits on the family until church is over. The next day is a work day. Dad's Father goes back to work. The weekend comes, and Dad's Father goes out for the night to meet his girlfriend.

DAD'S FATHER

Are you ready?

GIRLFRIEND 1

Yes.

Dad's Father is clean shaven with a clean suit and hat to match. A chocolate mulatto in the midst of the cotton fields. He left home driving a clean ride with the smell of sweet cologne. Dad's Father and his girlfriend make love near the tree by the window. After the date, Dad's Father returns home.

MaDear is silent.

Dad's Father says nothing to his wife — MaDear and goes straight to bed. He awakes the next morning and goes to work. At work, an 18-wheeler crashes the tractor trailer that he is on. Dad's Father dies on the tractor trailer.

SCENE 5

At the funeral, Dad has flashbacks about his Father's relationship with his girl-friend. Dad's Father liked his son's girlfriend. Dad goes back in time where he met his girlfriend near the tree by the window.

DAD (TO DAD'S FATHER)

I met a girl at school. I like her.

DAD'S FATHER

I want to meet her.

The next day, Dad asks the girl to come over his house. After school is over, Dad and the girl arrive at his house.

DAD

Here she is, Dad.

DAD'S FATHER

You are right, son. She is pretty. Here's a quarter. Buy her some candy.

DAD

Okay. I will.

The next day at school, Dad buys his girlfriend some candy. School kids are at play where the boys are running after the girls, grabbing at their ponytails. Dad's Girlfriend is eating the candy near the tree by the window

DAD

Can I walk you home?

They arrive at the house. Dad's Girlfriend introduces him to her parents. The girl's dad does not like him. Dad and his girlfriend meet at school again. Dad asks his girlfriend out for a movie. She tells him she would have to ask her parents. Her parents agree but tell her that she has to be at home at 10:30 p.m. They go to the movies but arrive home late.

SCENE 6

Near the tree by the window, Dad and his girlfriend make love. After sexual activity, Dad takes her home.

DAD

I had a nice time.

DAD'S GIRLFRIEND

Me too.

The Girlfriend's Dad comes outside, scolds him for being late, and tells him that he is not welcomed at the house anymore. One month later, Dad's Girlfriend realizes that she is pregnant.

DAD'S GIRLFRIEND (TO PARENTS)

I'm pregnant.

GIRLFRIEND'S MOM

What?!

DAD'S GIRLFRIEND

I'm pregnant.

GIRLFRIEND'S DAD

What did you say?

DAD'S GIRLFRIEND

I'm pregnant.

GIRLFRIEND'S DAD

I told you that boy was up for no good. I'm sorry; but you got to go and live somewhere else. Get Out!!!

Dad's girlfriend goes to MaDear's house to stay. MaDear welcomes her.

DAD'S GIRLFRIEND

I need a place to stay. I am pregnant.

MADEAR

That's fine. Now let's go outside and work in the truck patch field.

Before they go to the truck patch, MaDear opens the window and talks to her neighbor near the tree.

MADEAR

It's a nice day to work in the truck patch.

NEIGHBOR

Yes it is. We need the okra, purple hulled peas, corn, and the greens.

MADEAR

I'm waiting to receive a pound of ice cream.

NEIGHBOR

Is that right? We are milking the cow. Later we will churn the milk into butter and cheese.

Nine months later, Dad's Girlfriend has a baby boy. Dad and his girlfriend get married before the baby was born.

After Mom gives birth to a baby boy, she drops out of high school. Several months later, she gives birth to child 2. A year later, she gives birth to child 3

Scene 7

After working on the truck patch, they return home. Dad's sisters are in the house with Dad's kids. They are in the kitchen cooking.

MaDear

Hi kids.

Sister 1

Dinner's ready.

They eat dinner. Dad's sisters are upset with MaDear for letting her son's wife stay with them.

Sister 3

MaDear, why are you letting her stay with us?

MaDear is silent.

Sister 3

Well, she and the kids have to go.

Sister 2

I don't mind her staying with us

MADEAR (TO SISTER 3)

I'm sending you and your sister to college. There's enough room for me, my son, his wife and kids.

DAD (ENTERS)

I would like to go to college, MaDear.

MADEAR

You cannot go to college. I need your help in the truck patch.

A year later, Dad continues to help his mother with the truck patch. Dad is unhappy and starts to rebel against the family. Dad becomes rebellious along with his friends. Like his father, Dad goes out on the weekends and neglects his family. With the pressure and scrutiny from Dad's sisters and the neglect from her husband, Mom decides to move out of town. She packs her bags and gets the kids ready. They leave Dixie and move to Houston.

MADEAR (TO DAD)

Where is your wife?

DAD

I don't know.

MADEAR

She packed and her clothes are gone along with the kids. I remember her saying that she wanted to go to Houston, but I didn't know she wanted to stay in Houston.

DAD

It's my fault. I have been neglecting her and the kids. I lost my father, a friend, and now my family.

Dad begins to have flashbacks. He is afraid that his Friend 1 is out to get him. Dad chooses to leave Dixie to Houston. He leaves because he is running away from his friend. He does not leave because Mom left. He is running away from his friend who is now an enemy. Mom thinks that he wants to be reunited with her, but he is running away from the enemy. Dad is out of touch with reality. He is nervous and sweats profusely. He is ill and does not have a diagnosed illness.

DAD (TO SELF)

I am not feeling well. I can still hear the gunshots at the Gambling Shack. My dad is gone, I have lost a friend, and now my family.

Dad leaves Dixie to Houston. He finds his wife and kids. They move in a house in Houston

SCENE 8

Before Dad bought the house, he finds a job. His supervisor is difficult to work with. After a week's work, Dad goes out on the weekends.

DAD (TO MOM)

I'm going out tonight.

MOM

Okay. Bring some hamburgers back for me and the kids.

DAD

Okay.

Dad goes to the club for a drink. He drinks, loses track of time, and doesn't get the hamburgers. He returns home. Mom looks out the window near the tree and sees Dad slumped over the steering wheel. She manages to get him out of the car into the house.

DAD (HAS HANGOVER)

I feel sick all over. I'm sick.

The next work day, he goes to work.

SUPERVISOR

Cut these drill bits.

DAD

Okay. I am dusty with dust drill bits.

Five years later, Dad's friend gets out of prison. Friend 1 goes to MaDear's house.

FRIEND 1

I'm looking for your son. Where is he?

MADEAR

Leave him alone. He has nothing to do with you.

FRIEND 1

I am a changed man now. I'm out of prison. Your son was the best friend I ever had.

MADEAR

He no longer lives here. He moved to Houston, Texas.

FRIEND 1

I want to see him and make amends with him.

MADEAR

I'll give him a call and let him know you are looking for him. Just a minute. I'll give him a call.

DAD

Did you tell him where I live?

MADEAR

Yes. He told me he was a changed man.

DAD (NERVOUS)

MaDear, he won't ever change. Why did you tell him where I live?

MADEAR

It will be all right.

Friend 1 goes to Houston for revenge. He finds Dad at home and on the job. He talks to Dad's supervisor.

FRIEND 1

I'm looking for my friend who is an employee here.

SUPERVISOR

You're talking about crazy man—the mulatto.

FRIEND 1

Yes. He testified against me in court. I'm out to get him.

SUPERVISOR

That's good. I'll help you.

After MaDear calls Dad about his friend, Dad decides to move to another house. Six years pass and to this union five more children were born. A total of eight kids in a household of 10.

SCENE 9

Mom is pregnant with child 8. She kneels down praying to God for a baby girl.

MOM (KNEELING)

Dear God, please give me a baby girl.

God gives Mom a baby girl. They live in a household of 10 in a two bedroom/one bathroom house. Dad is overwhelmed with the household. Child 8 has grown to five years old. Now a child, she stands outside of the residence. In front of the house's front window near the tree, the child kneels down in front of the window scribbling on dirt in chicken scratch. She finds a gadget and plays with it. Friend 1 placed the gadget near the tree by the window. While outside, the wind blows dirt on her, and she hears a voice.

VOICE OF GOD

You are the solution and not the problem!

CHILD 8

What?

At Dad's workplace, Friend 1 meets with Dad's supervisor. They mastermind the gadget with dusty magnetic drill bits.

SUPERVISOR

The gadgets we use on him will put him in to shock.

FRIEND 1

Thanks for the gadgets.

Friend 1 goes to Dad's house and places another gadget near the tree by the window. Dad returns home from work. Child 8 reaches for him, grabbing his legs by the knees. She is like a leaf falling dizzily from a tree. Dad looks down at the child and shakes her off.

DAD (TO CHILD)

Not mine! You are not my child!

CHILD 8

Oh.

Child 8 starts to play with the gadget. The gadget puts Dad into shock. The gadget activates the magnetic dust clippings on Dad's body.

CHILD (TO SELF)

He says I'm not his. Whose am I? I don't know who I am. I am a nobody. And how can I be the solution? I am the baby of the family. I am too small and too young for this huge problem.

Child 8 becomes an Adult/Child. She is part child and part adult with a huge responsibility.

Scene 10

The Adult/Child plays with gadget while Dad is in the living room. He has a whole-body spasm with his hands tremoring. He goes to the back door of the house and opens the door.

DAD (TO SELF)

My supervisor and friend are my enemies. It is a threat. They are out to get me.

Dad's job goes out of business. He finds another job. While at home, he is ill. While the Adult/Child plays with gadget, Dad goes to the back door talking to himself. Mom notices his strange behavior and decides to put him into the hospital. He is placed in a strait jacket and goes to a mental institution.

PSYCHIATRIST (TO DAD)

How are you doing?

DAD

Not well. The enemy is out to get me.

PSYCHIATRIST

Who is the enemy?

DAD (NERVOUS)

My supervisor and my friend. I hear voices that tell me that they are out to get me.

The psychiatrist diagnoses Dad with a mental illness.

PSYCHIATRIST

Have you been in the hospital before?

DAD

Yes. I have flashbacks of the death of my father and a friend who killed a man. I still hear the gunshots that killed the man.

SCENE 11

Dad has a nervous breakdown in the hospital. His attire is off-white clothing. He looks out the hospital window near the tree and starts to hallucinate hearing voices.

DAD (TO VOICES)

No that's not my child. Not mine! That's not my wife. My supervisor is sweating me and my friend is out to get me!

Hospital assistants put Dad in a strait jacket to calm him down. Dad calms down. A month later, he is discharged from the hospital. Dad returns home. He does not acknowledge his wife and children.

CHILD 8 (TO MOM)

What's wrong with Dad?

MOM

He's sick.

CHILD 8

Like a cold or flu?

MOM

No. You wouldn't understand.

CHILD 8

Do you know how sick he is?

MOM

I think so.

DAD (ENTERS)

Get away from me!

CHILD 8

Okay. Okay. I'm not yours, and I don't want to be yours.

Dad is silent.

Child 8 is an Adult/Child. She becomes both an adult and child with arrested development and no personality.

ADULT/CHILD (TO MOM)

Mom, Dad says that I am not his.

MOM

That's what he says; but I know you are his.

ADULT/CHILD

Divorce Dad, Mom.

Mom is silent.

ADULT/CHILD

Divorce Dad, Mom. We can do without him. Maybe things will get better without him. Don't worry, Mom. I will help you.

MOM

I can't divorce him. But I will tell you why when you are older.

SCENE 12

Due to Dad disowning her, the Adult/Child was eager to go to school the next day. She felt better at school away from Dad and the house. At school, the teacher and students played a game. The students learned how to play the game 'make believe.' It was a game where one could pretend.

ADULT/CHILD (TO SELF)

I pretend that Dad is not my father. I have another father who is a rich man, smokes a pipe, and loves me unconditionally. I like school because I am away from home.

School ends and the Adult/Child returns to the house. She arrives home and sees Dad sitting on the couch. She does not speak to him and begins playing make believe.

ADULT/CHILD (TO SELF)

Dad, you are invisible!

The Adult/Child sees her created father in the place of Dad. She hallucinates and make believes. She feels better and never cries about Dad disowning her again.

ADULT/CHILD (TO SELF)

My dad gave me my name. I pretend that I have another name. My new name is Sydney. I will tell only one friend my created name. I want no parts of the name Dad gave me.

The Adult/Child thinks there is nothing wrong with pretending because it makes her feel better. Everything and everyone is make believe. The Adult/Child becomes confused and asks Mom some questions.

ADULT/CHILD

Why are things so bad? What's wrong with Dad?

MOM

I'll tell you when you are older.

Like her dad, the Adult/Child is ill. She hallucinates and has delusional thinking. Make believe, lies, and an undiagnosed illness keeps her in pain. Later, the Adult/Child finds out that playing make believe is lies. But make believe and lies were a way out. It was survival that shielded the Adult/Child's pain. Dad's verbal abuse towards her caused her not to know who she is.

SCENE 13

The Adult/Child's Mom tells her about the murder Dad was involved in.

ADULT/CHILD

Where was the murder scene located?

MOM

At the Gambling Shack near the tree by the window.

ADULT/CHILD

Mom, show me where it's located.

MOM

I will. The crime scene was at the Gambling Shack near the tree by the window.

The Adult/Child packs her bags; along with the gadgets Friend 1 placed there. She takes a trip to Dixie, LA, in search of herself.

ADULT/CHILD (TO MADEAR)

Hi MaDear

MADEAR

Hi.

ADULT/CHILD

I came here to find myself. I also want to go to the Gambling
Shack.

MADEAR

I'll show you where it's at; but I have nothing to do with it.

ADULT/CHILD

Okay.

MaDear shows the Adult/Child the crime scene. MaDear leaves the scene. The
Adult/Child stays at the scene. The child takes the gadget and carves the name
"Bradford" on the Bradford tree, and leaves in tears. The Adult/Child returns
to Houston, TX.

ADULT/CHILD (TO MOM)

Mom, what is the big family secret about Dad?

MOM

It is time for you to know why things are so bad. Your grandfather
was a hard-working sharecropper. He passed away and left your
dad with all the responsibilities. Your dad did not want to work in
the fields; but wanted to go to college.

ADULT/CHILD

I can imagine how bad he must have felt. The dreams of a better
life for himself is what he always wanted. How miserable he must
have felt about things going the other way.

SCENE 14

The Adult/Child was considered a "gifted" student. She was offered to go to an advanced school away from her neighborhood. The school in her neighborhood was considered "regular" for non-gifted students.

ADULT/CHILD (TO SELF)

I feel better leaving the house to go to school.

The child, now an Adult/Child went to Senior High School. She is an Adult/Child due to her arrested development and loss of a personality. School became difficult where she was unable to make believe. School was no longer a place of escape. As a result, she dropped out of school.

ADULT/CHILD (TO SELF)

I am in so much pain all over. I have no one to talk to. I have nowhere to go. This pain is too much to bear. What a senseless childhood!

Two years passed. The Adult/Child returned to Senior High School and received her diploma. After graduation, she went to the military.

ADULT/CHILD (TO MOM)

Mom, I'm going to the military.

MOM

Oh, no. I don't want you to go.

ADULT/CHILD

I'm going to find myself.

In San Diego, the Adult/Child served during the Persian Gulf War. After the war, she went to purchase a National Defense Medal at the Military Base Store. On the way to the store, she was involved in a fatal car accident. The accident was not her fault because she had the right of way. The other car hit her from the mid rear passenger side. Upon impact, she heard two voices.

VOICE OF GOD

Brace yourself back in the seat and hold the steering wheel tight.

VOICE OF THE ENEMY

You are mine now. You are going straight to Hell!

As the car rolled over, the Adult/Child thought she was going to die. She heard the voice of God.

VOICE OF GOD

I can't take you now. I know you never knew who your father was;
but today I tell you that I am your Father.

The Adult/Child survived the accident with no broken bones. God saved her life.

ADULT/CHILD

Lord God, you know that I was not ready to go to Heaven. I'm
crying because I am happy for a second chance.

The Adult/Child was delighted that God gave her a second chance. At that moment, she experienced a whole-body spasm.

Adult/Child

Thank you for saving my life.

The conversation with God continued near the tree by the window.

Voice of God

You have everything except a Holy Bible. You need one.

SCENE 15

The Adult/Child called her Mom from the hospital.

ADULT/CHILD

Hello, Mom.

MOM

Hello!

ADULT/CHILD

I'm calling to let you know that I was in a terrible car accident.

MOM

Are you all right?

ADULT/CHILD

Yes. I had a rollover accident in my car. My car flipped over. I survived the accident with no broken bones.

MOM

I know. I prayed to God to keep you from hurt, harm, and danger.

The Adult/Child experienced a whole-body spasm. In tears, she was grateful for her Mom's prayers.

ADULT/CHILD

Thank you, Mom. I'll call you later.

MOM

Okay. Goodbye.

The Adult/Child reported back to military duty. Her supervisor knew about the accident.

SUPERVISOR

I heard about the accident. Did you have on your seatbelt?

ADULT/CHILD

Yes, the seat belt saved my life.

SUPERVISOR

Well, I want you to teach us in training the importance of wearing a seat belt.

ADULT/CHILD

Okay.

A year later, the Adult/Child was honorably discharged from service. Before being discharged, she called her Mom.

ADULT/CHILD

Hi, Mom.

MOM

Hello.

ADULT/CHILD

I'm coming home this weekend.

MOM

Very well. Good.

ADULT/CHILD

It's your birthday—what do you want for your birthday?

MOM

Well, I want a pair of shoes.

ADULT/CHILD

No, Mom. What do you really want?

MOM

I really want a new home and not a house.

ADULT/CHILD

Okay, Mom we will find a home.

On her way home from San Diego to Houston, the Adult/Child had time to think and so many things to do. Although she knew who her ultimate Father was, she was still learning things about herself. She matured somewhat in the military, but remained an Adult/Child due to arrested development and the loss of a personality.

SCENE 16

The Adult/Child returned home and found a job in the federal service. She also attended college. These two occupations helped her buy a new home.

ADULT/CHILD (TO MOM)

I am going to search for a new home. Do you want to go with me?

MOM

Yes. I would love to go.

ADULT/CHILD

What kind of home are we looking for?

MOM

We're looking for a three bedroom, two bathroom with both formals and an attached garage.

ADULT/CHILD

All we need for us is a small home.

MOM

No. Let's get a home that is big enough.

ADULT/CHILD

Okay.

The Adult/Child and her mom moved into a new home not just a house.

MOM

I am so happy we found a new home. I thank God for you helping me. I prayed for a baby girl, and God gave you to me.

ADULT/CHILD

I wish I would have known this sooner. But I know God told me that I was not the problem, but the solution.

The Adult/Child found a job before buying a new home. She loved her job. A year later, she started to have job difficulty. She, too, had problems with her supervisor.

SUPERVISOR

Make me breakfast. I like soft bacon.

The supervisor brushed up against her breasts.

ADULT/CHILD

If I make you breakfast…you better be afraid to eat it.

The Adult/Child is sexually harassed. The supervisor made life on the job miserable.

SUPERVISOR

If you report that I sexually harassed you—you are going to lose your job.

The Adult/Child filed a sexual harassment claim. She went to the Union for help. The Union did not help her and wanted no parts of her claim. The Adult/Child sought medical attention. In tears, she was depressed.

ADULT/CHILD (TO PSYCHIATRIST)

I am depressed. I filed a sexual harassment claim while on the job, and I cannot return to that job location.

PSYCHIATRIST

I will write you a medical excuse that states to place you at another job location.

ADULT/CHILD

Okay.

The psychiatrist wrote several medical letters. Management ignored them all. The Adult/Child had a lengthy absence off the job. She had no income coming in. The Adult/Child had to tell her Mom that she was losing her job. Her job, like her Dad's became the "enemy."

ADULT/CHILD (TO MOM)

Mom, I am losing my job because I won't sleep with my supervisor.

MOM

There's nothing wrong with you standing up for yourself. Most women would fall for that.

Management sent the Adult/Child to another location. But it was a temporary position. After 30 days, she was told to go back to her original job location. The Adult/Child had a nervous breakdown on the work room floor. She was transported to the Emergency Room.

Adult/Child

I can't go back to work under that supervisor.

Psychiatrist

This medical letter states that you cannot work under that supervisor.

SCENE 17

The enemy (management) labeled the Adult/Child as a whistleblower. Like her Dad's enemies, the Adult/Child faced enemies of her own with employment. Like Dad's enemies, the Adult/Child's enemies used gadgets on her.

THE ENEMY

We need gadgets to get through to her. Nothing else will do. We have tried to get next to her with everything else. Electric tasers, fumes, and electronic tracking. One of these tactics will bring her down.

The Adult/Child went to work. In an isolated work area, the janitor placed chemical fumes in a bucket. The Adult/Child could not breathe. This was management's way of getting rid of her. With the loss of employment, her finances suffered. On the job, the Adult/Child experiences muscle spasms on her neck. The enemy aimed the gadget in her neck area. She went to the doctor, and the doctor said that she needed surgery.

ADULT/CHILD

I have pain on the back of my neck.

DOCTOR

I ordered an MRI. The X-rays show your brain stem is pressing against your spine. If you don't have the surgery, it may cause paralysis.

ADULT/CHILD

Okay. I will have the surgery.

The Adult/Child have surgery. Prior to surgery, the enemy replaced the surgical tray with a tray of gadgets. The surgeon unknowingly planted a bug in her head/neck area. The surgeon did not know that the surgical tray was tampered with.

THE ENEMY

Once the surgery is over, we will be able to gadgetize her.

The Adult/Child is discharged from the hospital. Upon her arrival home, she goes to her room to lie down. She experiences a whole-body spasm like her dad. Abruptly she gets up and goes to another room to lie down. In this room, she has another spastic episode. Unable to lie down on the bed, she decides to lie down inside the closet. In the closet, she has yet another whole-body spasm. She leaves the closet to recline in a chair. In the reclining chair, she gets some relief.

ADULT/CHILD (TO SELF)

I am in so much pain! Where is this pain coming from? I have one enemy that I know of. It must be them. They planted a bug in my head and inside the house. What am I going to do?

THE ENEMY (EAVESDROPPING)

She knows that she is bugged and the house is bugged. She is a whistleblower! She deserves to suffer.

SCENE 18

The Adult/Child files a sexual harassment claim. The claim angers management. Written correspondence creates a "paper war" near the tree by the window.

ADULT/CHILD (TO SELF)

I have to fill out this paper work. The claim must be filled out on time. If it is not filed on time, management will dismiss my claim.

MANAGEMENT

We will not tolerate this claim. But as long as she files the claim, we must respond to it. We must stop her!

One year later, the claim creates an enormous pile of paper. The Adult/Child was out of a job during the claim. The Adult/Child had no income coming in.

ADULT/CHILD (TO SELF)

How long will management improperly address my claim? Will I ever get my job back? I had surgery on my brain stem. I can't lift heavy packages. I am out of a job.

Before the Adult/Child loses her job, she returns to work where all of the odds are against her. Her supervisor returns to work when she returns to work at the same job location. She is being stalked by her supervisor. The Adult/Child leaves the job site and goes to the Doctor.

ADULT/CHILD (TO DOCTOR)

I returned to work and my supervisor followed me to work. I can't work under the pressure and scrutiny.

DOCTOR

Do not return there. I will write a medical release.

SCENE 19

The enemy starts to tailgate the Adult/Child wherever she goes. The Adult/Child looks out the rearview mirror. She sees an unmarked car following her.

ADULT/CHILD (TO SELF)

That's another supervisor harassing me. Their abuse of power is cowardly. I will not acknowledge her.

The supervisor follows the Adult/Child to the restroom, looking straight ahead. The supervisor makes sure that the Adult/Child sees her. This convinces the Adult/Child that the enemy is management. The enemy places an electric bug inside the Adult/Child's car. The Adult/Child is helpless.

ADULT/CHILD (TO SELF)

I am on medical leave. All of my medical letters are being ignored. I need an attorney to help me with my claim.

The Adult/Child consults with an attorney to see if it would help filing the claim. The attorney accepts the case and writes management a letter. The attorney tells the Adult/Child that he will have her claim properly addressed. The Adult/Child gives all her paper work to the attorney.

ATTORNEY (TO ADULT/CHILD)

Submit all the paper work to me. When you properly file a claim, you need legal assistance. With my help, management will properly address your claim.

Six months later, management agrees to give the Adult/Child's job back.

SCENE 20

The legal and medical letters are sent to management. Management agrees to give the Adult/Child's job back. But getting her job is the onset of other problems. The letters help her get her job back; management has no intentions for her to keep her job. The use of gadgets and other tactics make the Adult/Child's job difficult.

MANAGEMENT (TO SELF)

We will let her have her job back; but we will continue to retaliate against her. It's just a matter of time. She will realize that her job description is over. She will give up.

ADULT/CHILD (TO SELF)

I liked my job; but not anymore. I will continue to stand up for myself. I have to let the job go. Management can have my job. I am a winner. I stood up for myself as a woman. I stood as a lady on the job. Godspeed.

The paper work claim continues. The time comes when the legal and medical letters stop. The Adult/Child has medical and legal bills that she cannot afford. She requests to pay the bills in installments. It takes years to pay off the bills.

Scene 21

The Adult/Child is unaware of the gadget used on her dad. The gadget that she found was placed in the yard near the tree by the window that Friend 1 placed there. Her handling of the gadget activated electric shocks on her dad. She is unaware that the enemy's gadget was used on her dad. The audience knows what the Adult/Child doesn't know about the gadget's use. However, she is aware of the gadgets used on her. The gadgets and electric shock bugs are placed in her home and in her car that cause severe pain. The audience knows that the Adult/Child and her dad are both gadgetized.

Adult/Child (to self)

The enemy's abuse of power is being used on me. I wish I knew how they put me in so much pain. But I know that they are using something.

The enemy's retaliation continues. The claim of sexual harassment stopped her supervisor from harassing her.

Adult/Child (to self)

I have to contend with both sexual harassment and harassment by all the enemies.

The Adult/Child goes to run some errands. She gets on the freeway and is tail-gated by the enemy. She looks in her rearview mirror. She becomes dizzy. The enemy aims the gadget behind her head. She pulls over on the side of the road for relief. She becomes afraid to drive. This results in her going back home.

THE ENEMY

Bingo! We hit the nail on the head. She can't finish nothing that she starts to do. Let's give her a taste of her own medicine.

ADULT/CHILD (TO SELF)

I don't know how long this will last. But I am more than a conqueror. God will keep me from hurt, harm, and danger. He will keep me when I can't keep myself.

SCENE 22

Without a job and the loss of income coming in, the Adult/Child has nowhere to go. Time passes by. Her mom follows her routine by going to church on Sundays. She's attended this church for 22 years. The Adult/Child's dad began to follow her mom to church. Before following her to church, they got a divorce. The Adult/Child's dad retaliates against Mom.

MOM (TO ADULT/CHILD)

Your Dad followed me to church today. He was very disruptive during church service. I don't know why he is following me; but I am not comfortable. I need your help with him.

ADULT/CHILD

Okay. I will go to church with you next Sunday.

The next Sunday, the Adult/Child and her Mom go to church. Like clockwork, Dad is being disruptive. When church service is over, the Adult/Child and Mom discuss going to another church. Dad exits the church, flirting with women asking them if they needed a ride

DAD (TO WOMEN)

Do you need a ride?

ADULT/CHILD

Mom, you were right about Dad. He is an embarrassment the way he is acting. Together, we will find a new church home. He has the church members talking about you. We will find a church where he is unable to trespass against you.

MOM

Okay. That's a good idea.

The Adult/Child and her mom visit other churches. Finally, they find a church that they both like. The following Sunday, they visit the church of their dreams. It is a heavenly experience. They discuss the worship experience. They both agree to join.

The following Sunday, the Adult/Child joins the church. The following Sunday, her mom joins the church. Dad stops following her to church.

SCENE 23

MOM (TO ADULT/CHILD)

Thanks for your help finding us a new church home. We don't have to worry about your dad following us anymore.

ADULT/CHILD

You're welcome. There's a big difference with this church. They have security guards at this church. They didn't have security at the other church. It's a done deal. God told me that I was not the problem; but I was the solution. I enjoy helping you.

At the new church, the Adult/Child's mom sits beside the Pastor's Wife. The Pastor's Wife gives the Adult/Child's mom her phone number. The Adult/Child takes this to mean that she can talk to the pastor's wife like an open door policy.

ADULT/CHILD (TO MOM)

Mom, I am going to ask the pastor's wife for help. It seems like she is someone I can talk about my problems to. Give me her number. I want to talk to her.

The Adult/Child's mom gives her the phone number. The Adult/Child calls the pastor's wife.

ADULT/CHILD (ON THE PHONE)

Hello. I need to make an appointment for Christian Counseling.

PASTOR'S WIFE

Okay. Come on in. I'll be here.

The Adult/Child prepares to see the Pastor's Wife. Included in the preparation, she carries her resume to the appointment.

ADULT/CHILD

Thanks for the appointment. I need spiritual counseling. I don't trust medical counseling.

PASTOR'S WIFE

Wait a minute. You are going too fast. You may need both medical and spiritual counseling. What seems to be the problem?

ADULT/CHILD

The enemy is out to get me.

PASTOR'S WIFE

Who is the enemy?

ADULT/CHILD

I'm having problems with employment. I was sexually harassed by my supervisor. My supervisor is the enemy.

PASTOR'S WIFE

I have been sexually harassed, too. While I was in college, my professor made unwanted advances at me. It happens all the time. How can I help you?

ADULT/CHILD

I need a job. Here's a copy of my resume. Do you have any positions available?

PASTOR'S WIFE

I will have to ask the pastor if we have a job for you.

The meeting with the Pastor's Wife lasts for about an hour. The Adult/Child tells her about all of her problems. But the Adult/Child speaks about her problems too soon. The Pastor's Wife wants no part with the Adult/Child's problems. As a result, the Adult/Child was excommunicated from church. The Adult/Child believes that the enemy followed her to church.

SCENE 24

Due to being excommunicated from church, the Adult/Child stops going to church. But that doesn't stop her from taking her mom to church. The Adult/Child drops off her mom to church. After church, she picks her up.

ADULT/CHILD (TO MOM)

You know why I don't go to church.

MOM

Yes, I do. It reminds me of your grandfather. He dropped off his family to church and would stay outside until church service was over.

ADULT/CHILD

I cannot control following him in his footsteps. I hope it is not a curse.

After the Adult/Child found out that she was following in her grandfather's footsteps, she realizes that she is following in her dad's footsteps, too.

ADULT/CHILD (TO SELF)

My grandfather had problems with the clergy. My dad had problems with employment. Now, I am having problems with the enemy.

The enemy continues to retaliate the Adult/Child while going to church. The enemy tracks the Adult/Child while driving, at work, and her home. The enemy's gadgets used on her cause pain in her neck area, along with whole body spasms.

Years later, the Adult/Child realizes that the enemy is the reason behind Dad's illness. She also realizes that a different enemy targets her, too.

ADULT/CHILD

You (the enemy) attacked me and Dad at home and at work. You tried to destroy me; but you won't succeed.

SCENE 25

(SIX MONTHS LATER)

Gadgets are used by the enemy to keep the Adult/Child awake. After several days without sleep, the Adult/Child has a nervous breakdown. She has tactile and auditory hallucinations and starts to seek where the gadgets are located inside the home. She finds nothing visibly. She is unable to fall asleep due to electric shock sensations. She then attempts to rearrange furniture, pack her belongings, and place her belongings in her car. It is unclear where she would secure her belongings—unclear where she was going. The Adult/Child asks her Mom for help.

ADULT/CHILD (TO MOM)

I can't sleep! Help me! Please help me!

Due to insomnia, the Adult/Child is acting out of body, out of mind. She is acting irrationally like her dad. Her mom calls the police for help. The police arrive, and the Adult/Child resists being apprehended by the police. As a result, the police hogtie her ankles and take her to a mental institution to be observed.

ADULT/CHILD (TO MOM)

I asked for your help; not the police. Why call the police? They can't help me! Why are you doing this to me?

(TO POLICE)

Don't take me back to Dixie! Don't take me back there where the shooting occurred!

The Adult/Child hallucinates and sees things that are not there. She sees look-alikes of her mom and her doctors among others. She is under observation for half a day while the television is on. She is unable to understand the sequence of events on television because they are shown out of sequence; that confuses her. She discovers that her hospitalization is masterminded by the enemy. She stays in the hospital for a week during her birthday. The Adult/Child is convinced that the enemy masterminded her hospital stay.

ADULT/CHILD (TO PSYCHIATRIST)

It's my birthday and I am locked up in here. I don't want to be here.

The Adult/Child is discharged from the hospital with the diagnoses of schizophrenia.

ADULT/CHILD (TO MOM)

I remember when you admitted Dad in a mental institution. I want you to know that the enemy targeted Dad like they target me. But I know you don't understand. I am diagnosed with schizophrenia. Was Dad diagnosed with schizophrenia?

MOM

Yes.

Scene 26

The Adult/Child decides to stop seeking help. She begins to have flashbacks of her two occupations. She worked and went to college. In her senior year, she graduated from college. Later, she realizes that her matriculation in college was in vain because on senior picture day, she went to take her senior picture.

Photographer
You are going to remember this picture.

The photographer proceeds to take her picture. He put a Master's degree gown on her; instead of a Bachelor's degree gown. He knows that the Adult/Child is not on the Master's degree level. He knew what the Adult/Child didn't know. The photographer and the enemy is the cause for her picture not being shown in the graduation yearbook. It was also a way to show that the Adult/Child "mastered" all the enemy's plots against her.

Years later, the Adult/Child discovers that she is pictured in Master's degree gown rather than a Bachelor's degree gown. She decides not to request a refund for the graduation pictures. She places her picture on the fireplace mantel and leaves the matter alone.

Scene 27

Several years after graduation, the Adult/Child's dad died. She has the opportunity to forgive her Dad disowning her. While he was alive, she was unable to forgive him. His verbal abuse stunted her maturity. But at her Dad's funeral, she goes to his casket near the tree by the window.

Adult/Child (to Dad)

Dad, I want you to know that you are forgiven. I hope you made
it to Heaven.

The window of Heaven's sun rays permeate the funeral home. The voice of God speaks to the Adult/Child.

Voice of God

I know you have forgiven your dad. At your request, your prayer
has been answered. I told you that you are not the problem, but
the solution.

Forgiving her Dad is his ticket to Heaven. She does not want to hold her dad back from Heaven. At that instant, a burden is lifted off her shoulders. The Adult/Child's thoughts cleared. All of the things that her Dad said about her and the pain are reduced. Her dad's death makes the Adult/Child happy. God gives her strength, and this strength causes her to mature into an adult; no longer an Adult/Child. Finally, the Adult/Child matured to an adult.

Adult (to Dad)

Rest in peace! You don't have to worry about the enemies anymore. I have enemies like you did. We share the same illness. I was once an Adult/Child and was unaware of the enemies that pursued you. Now that I am an adult, I can face my enemies that target me.

The Adult/Child now an adult lives under the shadows of the enemy near the tree by the window. In her home, the adult looks out of the window in search of the enemy. The enemy plants bugs near the tree by the window. They trespass through the window looking in. The Adult closes the windows with curtains to keep the enemies from looking in.

SCENE 28

The Adult cannot convince anyone that the enemies were real. The Adult has flashbacks about her childhood. She remembers the game make believe as a child. Make believe helped the Adult in her youth; but later as time passes on, make believe is just a game. However, the Adult learned to believe. Just believe. Make believe as a fantasy; but to just believe is a reality

ADULT (TO SELF)

Now that I have matured into an adult, I have to believe that I can defend myself against the enemy. Now I have to learn how to live alone. My mom has decided to take a trip to Las Vegas.

MOM (TO ADULT)

I'm taking a trip to Las Vegas with my brother.

ADULT

No Mom, please don't go and leave me alone!

MOM

No, I don't see it like that. I need to take the trip.

Her mom leaves the Adult by herself all alone. This was the first episode of the Adult being left all alone to contend with the enemy. The Adult became afraid, but she remembers to believe that she can manage being alone. Her mom packs her bags and leaves to Las Vegas.

ADULT (TO SELF)

No matter what the enemies do, I will be looking through the window of Heaven. God is where the window of Heaven is.

SCENE 29

The Adult is not afraid of the enemy anymore. She realizes that the enemy will pursue her for the rest of her life. The bug in her head and at her home is permanent. Although she is not afraid of the enemy, she realizes that she would have to endure the pain.

(THE NEXT DAY)

The Adult doesn't sleep well. She awakes hallucinating, seeing a broken window. She calls the police, and the police don't find a broken window.

ADULT (TO SELF)

I have to fix these windows before Mom returns. Or should I just leave the windows as they are? I am not going to tell Mom about the windows. I'll just use curtains to hide the broken windows.

The Adult remembers to use her Bible. The Bible states that the windows of Heaven are a place of serenity. It is a place where God sees and knows all. A place where God pours out His blessings—a place of protection. It is a place where the enemy cannot go; a place of peace and quiet. Unlike the windows, the damaged windows near the trees are broken. The windows of Heaven shields the Adult from the enemy.

ADULT(TO SELF)

The windows of Heaven shines on me. It is God's promise to help me through difficulty. God give me strength.

The windows of Heaven shine on the trees. Once a tree is cut, it depicts annual rings—the age of the tree. The tree's significance when cut symbolize that the Adult is in a paper war with employment. Namely, these cut trees symbolize a waste.

The cut trees in Dixie and on the Adult's property foreshadow the enemy's retaliation. Near the tree by the window, the Adult retrieves a gadget at the old house. Her grandfather cut and cleared Bradford Pear trees in Dixie, and she cut and cleared trees near the tree by the window.

SCENE 30

The trees near the window in Dixie, Houston, and in Las Vegas are cleared and cut. The cut trees symbolize a 'paper war' and a waste of paper. The uncut trees symbolize old age. In Dixie, the cut trees are used for the daily newspaper. The Adult is told by her mom that Grandfather worked cutting and clearing trees. The Adult revisits the tree stump at the Gambling Shack. Bradford is carved on the tree stump by the Adult with the gadget that Friend 1 placed there. In Houston, the tree by the window remains uncut at the old house. At the new home, the Adult has the trees cut.

ADULT

I need my trees cut. The trees are blocking my view out of the windows.

TREE CUTTER

Okay. I will cut the trees. Do you want me to throw away the trees?

ADULT

No, don't throw away the trees. I need it as evidence. I have a file cabinet full of letters from the enemy. Now that I have turned all my paperwork to the attorney, I can burn all the trees and paperwork. But before I burn all of the paperwork, I will keep it for future reference.

In Las Vegas, like the Gambling Shack, patrons were at the slot machines. Mom does not gamble, but her brother does. There are cut trees in Las Vegas and a lot of windows. The enemy does not pursue the Adult's mom. Meanwhile, the Adult enjoys being alone. Instead of being bored, she keeps herself busy

ADULT (TO SELF)

Since I can't sleep due to the gadgets, I must go back to the places where I took pictures of the enemy tailgating me.

The Adult takes pictures of the trees and windows. She also takes pictures of her ankles to simulate them being hogtied. Then she goes to the camera shop to get the pictures processed. The enemy tailgates her to the camera shop. She stays in the camera shop for an extensive period of time wishing that the enemy would go away.

Scene 31

On her way to the camera shop, the Adult drove there ambulatory. The enemy tailgating her causes the car wheels to shake. She drives about 20 miles away from her home. She enjoys being in the camera shop and is eager to return home. But the enemy blocks all of the roads and freeways putting the Adult in traffic for an hour delay.

Adult (to self)

The enemy is the reason for the traffic. My drive home will take hours to get there. I'm the 'adult' who is stuck in traffic away from home. At the same time, I know that the enemy is trespassing inside my home while I am stuck in traffic. But there is nothing I can do about it.

After an hour, the Adult arrives home ambulatory. She goes inside the home looking for bug implants. She sees nothing visibly. So she decides to take a shower. She steps in the tub and feels grains of residue on her feet. Abruptly, she jumps out of the tub. She becomes nervous.

Adult (to self)

I feel grit under my feet. The enemy has been inside my home while I was at the camera shop. The grains in my tub feels like food seasonings. I have to check the kitchen.

The Adult checks the seasonings in the kitchen to see if they have been tampered with. She does not trust to consume the seasonings and decides to pour out all the grains down the drain.

ADULT (TO SELF)

I am afraid to consume the seasonings. I will get rid of all the old grains. I will buy individual packs of milk, juice, and bottled water. All seasonings are kept in individual packets. When I leave home, I will carry all the seasonings with me.

The Adult's purse was full with seasonings, a journal, and some books. She lived like a bag lady carrying everything in her purse. The bag was so heavy that the Adult gave up carrying the bag.

ADULT (TO SELF)

I can't go on like this. But I am not afraid. I will be careful what I eat in the pantry. I can't carry the whole pantry on my shoulders. I can't I can't pack my home on my shoulders.

SCENE 32

While the Adult was alone at home, she decides to get some film for her camera. She goes to the store, gets the film, and loads her camera. She stops on the side of the road and takes pictures of her commute. The first picture she takes is of the enemy. She turns to the back of the car and takes a picture of the enemy's unmarked car.

ADULT (TO SELF)

The pictures that I take will let the enemy know that I will not back down. When the enemy tailgates me, I will stop on the road and take a picture of the enemy's unmarked car.

The Adult makes it harder for the enemy to pursue her. As a result, the enemy begins to use different unmarked cars. She has the pictures processed and keeps them as evidence. She takes pictures while away from home. While she is at home, she purchases a video recorder and places it on the front window near the tree.

ADULT (TO SELF)

I am not going to allow the enemy destroy me. With my camera and video camera, I will catch the enemy in their tracks.

The Adult reviews the video daily. The enemy stops parking unmarked cars outside the home. The Adult reviews the video camera. Nothing suspicious is found on the camera. No activity outside the home was found. As a result, the gadgets that cause the Adult pain are reduced. Although the tailgating and pain are reduced, the Adult becomes weary.

ADULT (TO SELF)

I have not found no activity on the camera. Going over the evidence makes me weary. But I won't give up. The enemies are cowards.

SCENE 33

The Adult's mom returned home from the trip. She enjoys the trip. Her mom notices that in the kitchen the seasonings and liquids were in individual packets.

MOM (TO ADULT)

What happened in the kitchen?

ADULT

Nothing is wrong with the kitchen.

MOM

The gallon milk, juice, and water is bottled up and the seasonings are gone.

ADULT'

I decided to buy fresh seasonings and liquids. I hope you understand.

MOM

Okay.

The Adult did not share that the enemy was trying to poison her. Also, she did not share the incident with the damaged windows. The Adult poured the seasonings and liquids in the garbage disposal. Furthermore, her mom was given some fruits and vegetables from a church member.

MOM

These fruits and vegetables were given to me.

ADULT

Okay. I will put them in the refrigerator.

The Adult hears voices in her head that say the fruits and vegetables were tampered with. The Adult pours the fruits and vegetables down the drain. Later that evening, the Adult goes to the grocery store to replace the fruit and vegetables. The Adult realizes that she cannot trust anybody.

ADULT

What a relief that those fruits and vegetables are gone. I don't trust the enemy.

SCENE 34

The Adult decides not to tell her mom about the enemy. The Adult has to be strong enough to bear the enemy's evil ways.

ADULT(TO SELF)

I can't tell my mom that the enemy is trying to separate us. I have a lot bottled up inside. Mom does not know how much pain I am in. I got to be strong. I have no one to talk to but I won't give up. After years of pain, the Adult stands her ground resulting in the enemy becoming weary.

ENEMY (TO SELF)

She won't give up and we don't have the resources to continue harassing her. We have gadgetized her enough; but we know that she will have flashbacks of being gadgetized.

ADULT

What's going on? The pain has reduced. I will continue to stay the course and will not let my guard down. The enemy will not succeed destroying me.

Scene 35

The Adult has flashbacks of her childhood. Like her dad, the Adult and Child's attire are alike. The attire is off-white clothing. She goes back in time to reach for the Child's hand. She talks to the child.

ADULT

Reach for my hand and never let go. I put my arms around you in a place of safety.

CHILD

Okay. I'm just a nobody. Please help me!

ADULT

No. You are somebody. I have returned to you to let you know that you are growing up. Despite your loss of personality and arrested development, you can start being the adult you want to be. You have a right to be yourself—to just be you—a right to be free.

CHILD (IN TEARS)

I am in so much pain. I'm just a baby girl in the family. How can I help the family when I cannot help myself?

ADULT

Let's start with baby steps and take one day at a time. You have been chosen to help others. You help others well. Come to the light—that's where you belong. The light shines on you near the tree by the window.

CHILD

I want to talk to you; but I don't how.

ADULT

You can talk to me about anything. You are not alone. I am here for you. I've come back to save you.

The Adult goes back in time at her Child's early years. The location is at the hospital at the child's birth. Before her conception, her mom prayed for a girl. Mom is in labor with child. The camera lighting fades in from total darkness into yellow light, showing blood on the child (a close up shot) that symbolize iniquity.

After labor ends, Mom takes the child home. Mom rocks baby. After rocking the child, the child crawls away from Mom. (Dissolve lighting to total darkness.) Later the child has grown to five years old. The Adult lets the child know that she is there.

CHILD

I heard a voice in the wind near the tree by the window.

ADULT

Don't be afraid. The voice that you heard is from God. I love you. God loves you. Hold my hand and never let go.

Scene 36

The Adult and Child go back in time, holding hands, never to let go. The child remains in front of the Adult as a shield to protect the Adult. The Adult and Child are pursued by the enemy. The Adult explains to the child that she and their dad have enemies. They go back in time to hold their Dad's hand.

Dad's Spirit

Don't come back to hold my hand. Leave me alone!

The Adult, Child, and Dad are all dressed in off-white attire. They find their dad hallucinating near the tree by the window. He is wearing off-white briefs sweating profusely. The Adult and Child stands in the back of their dad. Their dad does not acknowledge them.

Adult

We've come back to tell you that the enemy cannot hurt you. We've come to hold your hand. We are here for you and not against you. We're here for support to let you know that you are not alone.

Dad's spirit goes back to the murder scene. The Adult and Child follow Dad. They are all afraid.

Child

I want to tell Dad to make believe.

Adult

That's a good idea; but make believe don't last forever. We have followed Dad's spirit to help him release the pain. We have taken him here so that he can become whole. Dad can wish the murder away. It was not his fault. He needs to know that we are on his side.

SCENE 37

The child asked the Adult, was it okay to make believe?

CHILD

Is it okay to make believe?

'ADULT'

It all depends. Make believe is just a game. Both of us has played that game; but it don't last forever.

The Adult and Child both in the same off-white attire go back in time. Their clothing (off-white) remains constant while the Adult and Child grow older together. The Adult follows the Child. The Child is in front of the Adult. The Child takes the Adult back to the tree by the window where she found the gadget that Dad's Friend 1 placed there. The Child asks questions.

CHILD (6 YEARS OLD)

I found this near the tree by the window. I was outside and the wind was blowing. I heard a voice in the wind. What does all of this mean?

ADULT (20 YEARS OLD)

I knew you would ask me. I've come to tell you that our Dad had enemies. The enemy placed the gadget there to harm Dad. The voice we heard was the voice of God. This means that we are protected from the enemy.

CHILD

What about the gadget?

ADULT

The gadget was used as a weapon against our Dad. Later, we found out that the gadget caused Dad to have whole body spasms. Dad could not help himself. He was afraid, alone, and confused. That is the reason why he disowned us and that is why we forgave him. Hold my hand. Trust me. Let go and let God.

The Adult and Child returns back to their home near the tree by the window.

SCENE 38

Near the tree by the window, the windows of Heaven shine on the Adult and Mom's home free of gadgets. God pours out blessings on the home. God's protection on the home is not lost. The Adult and Mom were blessed by God to pay off the home. The Adult had no income coming in. The Adult's mom's finances paid half the amount on the home and supernaturally paid the rest.

ADULT (TO SELF)

Lord, I thank you for being there every step of the way. You see how the enemy is trying to destroy me. Your arms of protection include me, my mom, and the home. I can do nothing without you. You have grace and mercy on everything that concerns me. Shine the windows of Heaven on me. I'm reaching for your hands— never to let go.

In their God given home, the Adult and Mom thrived as homeowners. Despite the enemy's pursuit, the Adult and Mom were protected by God.

MOM (TO ADULT)

It's peaceful living here. I want you to know how much I appreciate you helping me.

ADULT

I enjoy helping you, Mom. God told me to be the solution and not the problem. And I am here. I am free to do what God wants me to do. He has blessed us in a beautiful home and for that I am grateful. The enemy tried their best to separate us; but God said, "The enemy is defeated," as long as we stay on God's side.

SCENE 39

Years later near the tree by the window, the Adult hallucinates, finding all windows broken inside the home. The Adult has delusional thinking that the broken windows were caused by the enemy. The enemy violated the Adult's privacy looking in all the windows. The Adult hallucinates that the brick house is a glass house. The Adult becomes anxious and asks her mom to leave the house.

ADULT (TO SELF)

The windows are broken by the enemy. Our brick home is filled with broken glass. The enemy's last resort is to implode the house. Let's get out of the house and allow the enemy to destroy all the gadgets in the house. We will rebuild later.

MOM

I didn't know that the enemies were real.

Mom goes back in time when Dad was in a mental institution. The enemies that pursued Dad, Mom was unaware that the enemy caused Dad's strange behavior. She goes back in time to talk to Dad's spirit and asks for forgiveness.

MOM (TO DAD)

Forgive me for not being aware of the enemies pursuing you.

After Mom goes back in time, she returns to the glass house. Her daughter sees what her mom doesn't see—a glass house. The windows of Heaven shine on the glass house near the tree by the window. Mom apologizes to the Adult about the enemy. Mom is convinced that the Adult told her the truth about the enemy.

SCENE 40

The house is completely destroyed. The Adult writes a poem about their home.

"THE ENEMY'S HAND"

Before the 'adult's' journey
A gadget is embraced
Near the tree by the window
The sound of broken glass
From a distance is heard
From whence she lived
In her hand a gadget is loosely held
Under the sun glass shatters on the ground
On dirt, sand, and mud clay
As femme soles thrive in their God-given home
In the presence of God
As strands of female hair
To avenge the hand of the enemy

After the home is rebuilt, the Adult had a master plan concerning the enemy's trespassing.

ADULT

Mom, since we have rebuilt our home, I have decided to come against the enemy's trespassing. Someone needs to stay in the home, never leaving the home empty. If I go out of the home, you stay. If you leave, I'll stay in the house.

MOM

Okay. That's a good idea. We are a team that defeats the enemy.
We are together as one.

The master plan works, keeping the enemy at bay. The Adult keeps the enemy under control. With all the gadgets destroyed in the home, the Adult feels better. The enemy could only target the Adult's car near the tree by the window.

The home was rebuilt with love protected by God. The Adult and Mom proved to be a team committed to the house that became their home. A home rooted on a firm foundation. The enemy targeted the wrong home. The enemy cannot break the Adult and Mom's relationship. The Adult is grateful that her Mom understands that the enemy is real.

SCENE 41

The Adult needs an outlet. She had few associates to be with—to talk to. The associates she has go out on the weekends with her. They go to the night club, dancing the night away. At the club is a place to get away and fantasize. Like the game make believe, the club patrons take on a double identity.

ADULT (ON THE PHONE)

Hello. Let's go out tonight.

ASSOCIATE

Okay. How will we get there?

ADULT

We'll catch the bus and worry how we get back later.

ASSOCIATE

Okay. Let's go.

The Adult and Associate went to the club. It's cold outside. For hours, the Adult and Associate danced into a sweat all night long. When the club closed, the Adult and Associate did not have a way home. They walk several miles to get home. Away from the club, they resort to being their true selves.

ASSOCIATE

It's cold out here and we have miles to go. This is crazy!

ADULT

Yeah. This is crazy. But we had fun! This is fun!

ASSOCIATE

Yeah. We did have fun…have you read the book, *The Longest Mile*?

ADULT (LAUGHING)

No, I haven't.

ASSOCIATE

Well, we have the longest mile to go.

ADULT (LAUGHING)

Oooh! It's cold.

The Adult and Associate left the club at 2:00 a.m. They made it home in three hours. The long walk made them hungry. So the Adult made them something to eat.

SCENE 42

On the weekends, the Adult goes to the club to dance the night away. The night club had 'mask night,' where the patrons wore masks. It's fantasy night where patrons pretend to be someone else. With their masks on, each patron has an identity different from their true identity. It's a form of make believe. The Adult uses the name 'Sydney' as her double identity. Some patrons are happy and some are sad. It's hard being their true selves during the week. All of the patrons have issues. Some of the patrons are disowned by their parents. Some are verbally and physically abused brought up in a single headed household. The patrons that were neglected by their parents have problems being their true self. The club was an escape from reality. It was a place like their second home.

ADULT (TO SELF)

This club is my second home. A place that I lay to rest all my fears.

However, the Adult stops going to the club. She becomes whole and does not like fantasizing anymore. Her home is better than the club. The Adult matured into her true being.

Scene 43

With God's help, she prays to God that the enemy will not tamper with her finances. And like a whirlwind, she receives back pay in the mail that God allows her to have. The Adult is elated with her finances being restored.

ADULT (TO MOM)

Mom, I received a check in the mail. It is a miracle!

MOM

With all the things you've been through, you deserve the blessings. Everything that the enemy has put you through, you deserve many more blessings.

ADULT

I receive the blessings. God is for me and the enemy is against me. I am not on the enemy's side. The enemy can't do me no harm.

With her finances restored, the Adult was able to write about her life experiences. The screenplay is about a child who is disowned by her biological father that causes her to experience arrested development and no personality. When the Adult/Child reaches adulthood, she is both part child and part adult.

Throughout her life, she is targeted by the enemy. Although pursued by the enemies, she manages to overthrow them. As a whole Adult, the enemy continues to harass her. The Adult realizes that she will have to contend with the enemy for the rest of her life. The Adult continues to lead a life under the shadows of the enemy.

The Adult's life remains guarded near the tree by the window.

THE END